DATE DUE			
✓	✓		
✓	✓	net 3/8/10	
✓	✓	✓	
✓	✓	✓	
✓	✓	✓	
✓	✓	✓	
✓	✓		
✓	✓		
✓	✓		
✓	✓		
✓	✓		

Jenn'ifer

Carrie Measures Up

by Linda Williams Aber
Illustrated by Joy Allen

The Kane Press
New York

For Hal
—L.W.A.

Book Design/Art Direction: Roberta Pressel

Library of Congress Cataloging-in-Publication Data

Aber, Linda Williams.
    Carrie measures up!/Linda W. Aber; illustrated by Joy Allen.
    p. cm. — (Math matters.)
    Summary: Carrie measures all sorts of things to help her grandmother with her knitting projects and then Carrie decides to knit something special herself.
    ISBN-13: 978-1-57565-100-2 (pbk. : alk. paper)
    ISBN-10: 1-57565-100-9 (pbk. : alk. paper)
    [1. Measurement—Fiction. 2. Knitting—Fiction. 3. Grandmothers—Fiction.]
    I. Allen, Joy, ill. II. Title. III. Series.
    PZ7.A1613 Car 2001
    [E]—dc21   00-043819
                                                          CIP
                                                          AC

10 9 8

First published in the United States of America in 2001 by Kane Press, Inc.
Printed in Hong Kong.

MATH MATTERS is a registered trademark of Kane Press, Inc.

www.kanepress.com

Spiffy is getting nose marks all over the window, but I don't mind. He's helping me watch for my grandma. She's coming to visit for two whole weeks!

3

Spiffy is a great look-out. He never blinks.
"Keep watching, Spiffy," I say. I try on some
sweaters. I want to wear one Grandma
made, but it's so hard to choose!

Grandma's a knitter. She takes her yarn and her needles wherever she goes. Everybody in my family has tons of things she's made. Even Spiffy!

I sure wish I could knit like Grandma does. She says she'll teach me someday. I can't wait.

"Ruff, ruff, ruff!" Spiffy barks.

"Grandma's here!" I shout. I run downstairs and open the door.

"Hello, Sweetie!" Grandma says. She has a suitcase and, naturally, her BIG knitting bag.

After all the hugs and hellos, Grandma
settles down in her favorite chair. She
calls it her "sit-and-knit chair."

"*Tah-dah!*" she says. Then she gives me
a purple purse, a dress for my favorite
doll, and a funny, floppy hat. "Everything
is fantastic!" I tell her.

Grandma's knitting needles are already clicking away. "Can you give me a job to do?" I ask. I like to help Grandma.

"You can be my measuring spy!" she says.

"You mean sneak around and measure when nobody's looking?" I ask.

"Right!" says Grandma. "That way my presents will be real surprises." She hands me a bright blue tape measure. "You'll need this."

I unroll the tape. "It's long—seventy-two inches!" I say. "Can I start measuring now?"

Grandma
Knitting
List

Before Grandma can answer, Dad yells,
"Has anyone seen my other slipper?"
Spiffy races by—with Dad's slipper.
"Oh, no!" Grandma says. "Put slippers
for Dad at the top of our knit list!"

Here comes the measuring spy! I peek into the den. Perfect! Dad's reading. I crawl over and measure. Eleven-and-a-half inches. Dad's feet are just one-half inch less than one foot! That means his foot is less than a foot!

Being Grandma's measuring spy is fun. When nobody's looking, I measure everything on Grandma's list.

I measure Spiffy for paw warmers.

I measure my baby brother for tiny baby mittens.

I measure Mom's
laptop for a new
carrying case.

I measure the door
knocker. Grandma
wants to make a door-
knocker cover for
quieter knocks!

Then I kind of get carried away.
I measure everything in sight.
I'm a measuring maniac!

Mom would love a TV cover.

A bowling ball bag for Dad?

A hammock would be nice.

How about curtains for the birdhouse?

"Whoa!" Grandma finally says. "My knitting will never keep up with all your measuring. It's time for you to learn to knit!"

At last! I am so excited I can hardly talk.

"Let's head right over to the Yarn Barn," Grandma says.

What a great place! It's jam-packed with
cool knitting stuff! By the time we leave,
I have my own knitting bag, needles, and
balls of yarn—Cherry Red, Sunburst Yellow,
and Popping Purple.

At home Grandma shows me two knitting stitches, knit and purl. It looks easy. But it isn't! I keep trying. Little by little my knitting gets better.

Grandma always says that knitting
helps her think. She's right! I get a great
idea. "Grandma knits for everyone but
herself," I say to Spiffy. "So I'm going to
knit a scarf for Grandma. Her birthday
is only one week away!"

Of course, I have to follow Grandma's
rule, "Measure first, knit later." I wait
for Grandma to take a nap. Soon she
closes her eyes. Her knitting drops onto
her lap. She's asleep.

I drape the tape measure around Grandma's neck, just the way a scarf goes. It looks too short. I unroll the tape a little more. "Forty-five inches seems pretty good," I whisper to Spiffy.

I take out some Cherry Red yarn. I
decide to make the scarf eight inches
wide. Then I roll out the tape measure to
forty-five inches—just to see how much I
have to do. "Gee," I think. "That's a lot of
knitting!"

I knit for what seems like a long time.
Then I measure.

I work harder...

and harder!...

"No more measuring," I decide. "I'll just knit, knit, knit!"

I knit while I watch TV.

I knit while I watch the baby.

I knit on the school bus.

I even knit while my mom takes a splinter out of my big toe! Ouch!

It's the day before Grandma's birthday.
My fingers are very very tired. I can't
knit much more.

I decide I'd better measure the
scarf again. Wow! It's longer than
the tape measure! Oh, well. Better
too long than too short!

Then it hits me. How do I end the scarf?
That's one thing Grandma didn't teach me.
   Finally I put the scarf, needles and all,
into a big box. I wrap it up—and tie it with
the tape measure!

The big day is here. "Happy Birthday, Grandma!" I say.

Grandma opens the box. She takes the scarf out . . . and out . . . and out . . .

"It's beautiful—and so long! It's the longest scarf I've ever seen!" she says. "And, oh my, the knitting needles are still in the end!"

"I didn't know how to finish it," I explain. Grandma shows me just what to do.

"All done!" she says. "It's a scarf like no other scarf in the world! It's a scarf made for two! Let's go for a walk. I want to show it off."

Grandma throws the scarf around her neck—and around mine, too!

"I guess we'd better take a very long walk," I say, "to show off such a very, very, VERY long scarf!"

LENGTH CHART

Each piece of knitting yarn is a different length.

The red piece is about one inch long.

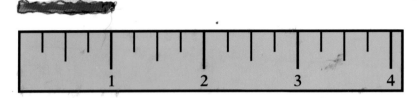

The blue piece is about one-and-a-half inches long.

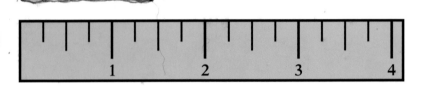

The yellow piece is about three-and-a-half inches long.

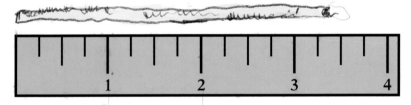

REMEMBER

Twelve inches equal one foot.   12 inches = 1 foot

Three feet equal one yard.   3 feet = 1 yard